KU-154-177

Are you ready to meet

# MISS PETULA
## PERPETUAL-MOTION?

**SEARCH AND FIND:**
What is the name of Petula's school?

Answer on page 60

# Miss PETULA Perpetual-Motion

THIS IS THE STORY OF A GIRL who would **not** sit still. *Miss Petula Perpetual-Motion* was forever in motion. Whether she was in a lesson, in church or even playing Musical Statues, some part of her would always be **moving**. It might be her foot, or her arm, or even her entire body.

It would start with

a little wiggle, then

become a waggle,

before turning

into a jiggle and

progressing to a JOGGLE.

Next she would be cartwheeling across the room, creating pandemonium wherever she went.

Petula was even in motion as she slept. Sometimes the other girls at her posh boarding school, $\boxed{\textit{Modesty Place}}$, would hear a noise in the dead of night. They would peek out from under their bedcovers and see Petula ballet-dancing across the dormitory with her eyes closed.

One day, Petula's rather grand headmistress announced that the girls of $\boxed{\textit{Modesty Place}}$ were to go on an awfully special trip.

"Quiet, girls!" ordered the lady as she stood on stage at assembly. Miss Prigg's grey hair was styled in a magnificent bouffant hairdo and a pair of half-moon spectacles hung from her neck on a gold chain. If she was about to tell someone off (which was often), the spectacles would be lifted up to her eyes so she could stare her victim down and give them the *willies*.

"Now, girls, we are going to take a school trip to somewhere I – your beloved headmistress – have chosen myself. We are going to visit my favourite **PORCELAIN** museum.

Needless to say, I expect you to be on your absolute best behaviour. I don't want any mishaps."

Suddenly all eyes were on Petula.

**OH NO!** thought the *good* girls sitting in the front row.

**OH YES!** thought the *bad* girls sitting in the back row.

To make matters worse (or better, depending on whether you were a good or bad girl), Petula was bouncing up and down on her seat like it was a space hopper.

BOING!

BOING!

BOING!

"**PORCELAIN** has long been a personal passion of mine," continued the headmistress, who loved making lengthy speeches. "Now I – your beloved headmistress – want to share that passion with you. This museum is the best in Europe. Every single piece on display is a priceless antique. There shall be no *'accidents'*. Do I make myself clear?"

There was a faint murmur from the pupils.

"I SAID, DO I MAKE MYSELF **CLEAR?!'** she bellowed.

"**Yes,** Headmistress," chimed the girls in unison.

"Excellent! Now, *Miss Petula Perpetual-Motion*, I need to see you in my study right away."

The girl glowed as red as a tomato driving a fire engine. What had she done wrong now?

Surely the time when she accidentally spun backwards into the Science block had been put behind her? Yes, the experiment taking place that day went badly wrong. Yes, there was still a huge hole in the floor where the acid burned through it. But Petula swore it was an accident.

Yes, her triple jump on sports day became an *octuple* jump (taking in eight different moves) and resulted in Petula karate-kicking the local mayor, sending him tumbling **off** the winners' podium.

But again the girl insisted it was an **accident**.

And yes, **of course**, who could forget the time at the school Christmas Carol Concert when Petula couldn't stand still in church, **cartwheeled** up the aisle and sent the vicar **flying headfirst** into the choir?

But these were **all accidents**.

It wasn't her **fault** she couldn't sit still.

Petula even had a note from her **mother** to prove it.

To Whom it may Concern,

My Darling Daughter, Miss Petula Perpetual-Motion, cannot stay still for more than a second. It is not her fault so she must not be punished in any way if she causes damage to property, buildings, people or animals. Please take great care of my Darling Daughter.

Yours truthfully,

Petula's mother

With some trepidation, the girl knocked on the door of the headmistress's study.

KNOCK KNOCK KNOCK!

"Come!" barked the headmistress from inside.

KNOCK KNOCK KNOCK KNOCK!

Petula's hand did not stop knocking.

"I SAID, **COME!**" came an angry-sounding voice.

Still Petula couldn't stop her hand from knocking.

KNOCK KNOCK KNOCK KNOCK KNOCK KNOCK KNOCK KNOCK!

"Oh, for goodness' sake!"

roared the headmistress.

Miss Prigg yanked open the door and Petula KNOCK-**KNOCK**-KNOCKED the lady slap-bang on her nose.

"Ow!" BOINK!

"Sorry, Miss Prigg," replied the girl with a hint of a smile. It was amusing to see the lady fuming.

"COME INTO MY STUDY

THIS INSTANT!"

ordered the headmistress.

Petula **forward-rolled** into the room, which Miss Prigg always had kept spotless. In fact an old cleaner was in there at that moment, busily polishing some school trophies on a table.

"You – out!" ordered the headmistress. Miss Prigg was curt to anyone she considered below her.

The cleaner picked up her dusters and shuffled towards the door.

"Quickly!" shouted Miss Prigg, and the poor old dear picked up her pace until at last she disappeared.

"Now, take a seat, *Miss Petula Perpetual-Motion,*" said the headmistress.

Petula did just that. She took a seat, and **danced** around the study with it.

"I meant, sit down!" barked Miss Prigg.

The girl whisked and whirled the chair to the floor, and slowly lowered herself on to it.

As soon as her bottom touched the chair she felt an overwhelming urge to bounce up and down on it, so she did.

"Be still!" demanded Miss Prigg. But Petula continued to bounce up

and d$o^wn$, the chair squeaking along
rhythmically with her **bounces**.

**BOUNCE**
   SQUEAK!

**BOUNCE**
   SQUEAK!

**BOUNCE**
   SQUEAK!

"Now, needless
to say, I want
you on your
absolute best
behaviour during
the school trip."

"Of course, Miss Prigg.
As if I would be
anything else."

**BOUNCE**
   SQUEAK!

**BOUNCE**
   SQUEAK!

The headmistress was not convinced. She lifted her half-moon spectacles up to her eyes and studied the girl.

"The truth is, you have left a trail of **destruction** behind you wherever you've been at [ *Modesty Place* ], which is the finest girls' boarding school in the country. I hardly need remind you of the **incident** in the school dining hall yesterday lunchtime. You began by juggling huge

bowls of **trifle.** Before long they were
z z z o o o o m i n g through
the air, heading
straight for the **teachers'** table."

"At least it saved you all the bother
of queuing for dessert, Headmistress,"
replied the little girl. If this was
designed to stop Miss Prigg from
becoming further enraged, it failed
**miserably.**

"I WAS COVERED FROM **HEAD** TO **TOE** IN **TRIFLE!**"

boomed the headmistress, her face now
boiling with fury, her teeth on the verge
of gnashing. "Only this morning I found
a piece of *jelly* in my ear."

"Did you eat it, miss?" enquired the
girl politely.

"**No!** I did NOT eat it!"

BOUNCE BOUNCE BOUNCE
SQUEAK! SQUEAK! SQUEAK!

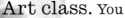

This noise was really distracting
the headmistress now, but she
pressed on.

"Then there was the time
you caused chaos in your
Art class. You

jiggled and wiggled and, before we knew it, there was paint sprayed across the walls, windows and ceiling…"

"Our Art teacher, Miss Splurge, remarked that she actually rather liked the redecoration."

The headmistress chose to ignore this *smarty-pants* reply.

"And the time when you managed to release ALL the lacrosse balls from the games cupboard. Miss Heft, your poor PE teacher, wobbled over and was carried off down the pitch on a sea of them!"

"I do hope they eventually **find** her," remarked Petula.

"I DO TOO!" bellowed the headmistress.

BOUNCE    BOUNCE    BOUNCE

SQUEAK!    SQUEAK!    SQUEAK!

Miss Prigg couldn't take it a moment longer.

**"WILL YOU BE STILL?!"** she ordered.

"Sorry, miss," muttered the girl. For a moment Petula was still. But the moment soon passed.

There was a wobble, then a wibble, ending up in a huge wubble. The girl performed a dive roll on to the floor, before finishing her acrobatics display with a handstand.

"Now, *Miss Perpetual-Motion*," purred Miss Prigg with a new hint of menace in her voice, "I need the trip to the **PORCELAIN** museum to pass without incident or ⟨ Modesty Place ⟩ – founded one thousand years ago by a nun, no less – could become a laughing stock."

"Of course, miss," said the ᴺᴹᴼᗡ-ƎᗡISԀՈ girl, who was now scuttling about the

headmistress's office
on her hands like
a **performing
poodle.**

"So I have ordered
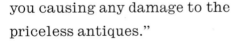's
Science teacher,
Professor Blink,
to come up with a
**contraption** to stop
you causing any damage to the
priceless antiques."

**Miss Petula Perpetual-Motion** did not like
the sound of this at all. "I will be fine
without it, thank you, miss," she said.
The girl's legs were now doing SCISSOr
kicks.

As she spoke, her legs sent a pile of school reports
flying off the headmistress's desk.
They looked like a flock of seagulls taking flight.

"No, you will not!" barked the
headmistress.

"What is this **contraption**, miss?"

"Oh, you'll see!" said Miss Prigg
ominously, desperately trying to pluck
the sheets of paper from the air.

"NOW GET OUT!"

With that, Petula cartwheeled out of the study, booting the newly polished trophies to the floor as she went.

CRASH!
BANG!
WALLOP!

\* \* \*

The day of the school trip arrived, and Professor Blink proudly wheeled her **invention** out of the Science block and into the playground.

"There we are, Headmistress!" said the lady, still sporting her white lab coat and safety goggles. "Just as you asked."

"It's **marvellous**, Professor!" replied Miss Prigg.

It looked like a giant **toy** for a hamster.

The Science teacher had created a huge, round, see-through inflatable ball, large enough for someone to be placed inside. Of course, that someone was **Miss Petula Perpetual-Motion**.

"I am proud to finally unveil my invention!" announced the professor. "I have named it the

## Bouncing BOOM-BOOM Ball.

"It is destined to stop jiggling children all over the world from destroying everything in their paths."

"KEEP IT BRIEF!" ordered the headmistress, who only liked the sound of her own voice.

"Yes, yes, Headmistress," replied the Science teacher hurriedly. "It's very simple – the child who **cannot stay still** is stuffed in here," she began, indicating a small hatch in the ball. "Then, when the child does fidget, the Bouncing **BOOM-BOOM** Ball will simply bounce off any precious objects nearby, causing **zero** damage."

At least that was the idea.

# "Splendid!" said the headmistress.

# "You may go!"

It was a long coach ride to the **PORCELAIN** museum. Despite the driver's protestations, the headmistress insisted that Petula travel in the boot so she couldn't cause any damage on the way.

As soon as they arrived, the headmistress stuffed *Miss Petula Perpetual-Motion* into the Bouncing **BOOM-BOOM** Ball. Then she led her party of schoolgirls inside the museum as Petula bounced along, bringing up the rear. Despite her initial reluctance, once inside the Bouncing **BOOM-BOOM** Ball the girl began to enjoy it. A smile spread across her face.

The museum was a treasure trove of all things **PORCELAIN**.

Porcelain *dogs*,
porcelain *cats*,
porcelain *plates*,
porcelain *vases*,
porcelain *teapots*,
porcelain *candlestick
holders*,

porcelain *porcelain*.

Every single object was an antique

and worth
a **fortune**.

"Now, girls, needless to say, there
is absolutely **no** touching of any of
the items on display," announced the

headmistress. "I know most of your mamas and papas are filthy rich since they send you to ⟨ *Modesty Place* ⟩, which I am proud to say is the most **expensive** school in the country. However, if you do touch anything and cause it to break, you will have to pay for it yourselves, every last penny. Does your beloved headmistress make herself clear?"

The pupils murmured.

"I SAID, DOES YOUR BELOVED HEADMISTRESS MAKE HERSELF CLEAR?!"

"Yes, miss," replied the girls.

"Now gather round!"

The girls huddled round a plinth. On it sat a large bowl, with

hundreds of tiny flowers hand-painted
round the outside. Petula bounced up
and down in her giant ball to try to
get a better look. Miss Prigg raised
her half-moon spectacles to her eyes.

"This bowl was made in Paris. It
once belonged to the last queen of
France, Marie Antoinette, and dates
back to the eighteenth
century."

Suddenly, in her eagerness to see, *Miss Petula Perpetual-Motion* bounced so hard that the Bounc<sup>i n g</sup> **BOOM-BOOM** Ball hit the ceiling.

From there it rebounded, gathering speed at an alarming rate.

WHAM!

BOOM!

BOOM!

Now it was going

up and down, up and down, up and down,

shaking the room as it b<sup>o</sup>u<sup>n</sup>ce b<sup>o</sup>unce

bounced.

The headmistress gasped

in horror. **Miss Petula**
**Perpetual-Motion** was
bouncing dangerously
close to the priceless
**PORCELAIN** pieces.

As the Bouncing **BOOM-BOOM**
Ball bounced closer and closer, Miss
Prigg stretched out her long thin arms
and gave it a shove. This caused the
contraption to start ricocheting off
the walls. As all the other schoolgirls
watched with their mouths open, it
walloped off the priceless **PORCELAIN**
without damaging it at all, and then
bounced back into the headmistress –

# BASH!

– sending her tumbling into a

**PORCELAIN** penguin

posing on a plinth.

"**Noooo!**"

she screamed.

The penguin went **flying** through the air.

It was an **unusual** sight as penguins are, of course, flightless birds. But the wonder of seeing such a bird finally taking flight was soon brought to an abrupt halt. The **PORCELAIN** penguin **smashed** against the wall…

CRASH!

...shattering into hundreds of tiny pieces. All the schoolgirls gasped in horror and **delight**.

"You'll pay for that, *Perpetual-Motion!*" shouted the headmistress.

"But I didn't touch the priceless **PORCELAIN**, Headmistress! You did!" reasoned the girl.

Needless to say, this made Miss Prigg blaze with rage. She chased after *Miss Petula Perpetual-Motion* as the girl bounce-bounce-bounced off to the other side of the room.

BOOM! BOOM! BOOM!

The headmistress raced towards the Bouncing **BOOM-BOOM** Ball, this time with her arms and legs outstretched to stop it. But, as it bounced off the wall, it sent the lady flying backwards through the air once more.

**THWACK!** The first thing she hit was a **PORCELAIN** statue of a *swan*.

**SMASH!** The second thing was a life-sized **PORCELAIN** statue of a *ballerina*.

**BANG!**

The third thing she hit
was a **PORCELAIN** statue
of a *clown*.

WAL LOP!

It wasn't one of those **happy** clowns. It was one of those sad clowns. Sadly there isn't time to fully explore the clown's emotional state. That's because said clown, along with those other objects flying through the air, was soon nothing more than a **shower** of **PORCELAIN** scattering across the floor.

# SHATTER!

At this very moment, hearing all the commotion, the elderly museum director came dashing out of his office. He popped his monocle into place to survey the damage. Every single one of the museum's most priceless pieces of **PORCELAIN** was in pieces.

"What is the meaning of this?!"

he bellowed, waving one of his walking sticks aloft in fury.

The headmistress wobbled to her feet, crunching **PORCELAIN** gravel underfoot as she did so.

**CRUNCH.**

**CRUNCH.**

**CRUNCH.**

"I can explain!" pleaded the lady.

"Who touched the precious, **priceless**, pleasing **PORCELAIN** pieces?" demanded the museum director.

"Well..." The headmistress glanced over at *Miss Petula Perpetual-Motion* who, to her surprise, was now bouncing only very gently in her plastic ball.

"Well, technically it was ME, but—"

"No buts!" shouted the museum director.

"Lady! **You** will pay for every last piece!"

"NooooooooooooooooooooooooooooOOOOO!!!"

screamed the headmistress.

The girl who couldn't keep **still** smirked.

\* \* \*

The museum's bill came to many **millions.** On a headmistress's salary, even at the most expensive school in the country, it would have taken a **thousand years** for Miss Prigg to pay everything back. So she had to take on lots of other jobs at Modesty Place .

Despite being a very grand woman, the headmistress now had to be up at dawn every morning with a mop and bucket, **cleaning** the school corridors.

At lunchtime she would be dishing out soup in the dining hall.

And after school most days, Miss Prigg could be seen up a ladder, clearing wet leaves and dead pigeons from the guttering.

And if there was one person **guaranteed** to

**KICK** over the

headmistress's *bucket*,

send the *soup*

**FLYING**

through the air,

or **TRIP** over

her *ladder*,

it was of course...

## Miss Petula Perpetual-Motion!

\*   \*   \*

Some years later it was Petula's very **last** day at ⟩ *Modesty Place* ⟨. She was eighteen years old now, and ready to somersault off into the world.

That morning the headmistress had been up at dawn **unblocking the toilets** and she had been called to the library to clear up some vomit after the librarian had come down with food poisoning.

As Miss Prigg angrily plonked down her mop and bucket, she spotted her **nemesis**, Petula, sitting in a corner of the library reading a book.

The strange thing was that the girl was sitting perfectly **motionless**.

Miss Prigg hid behind some shelves of books, and spied on her most-hated pupil. Apart from turning a page every couple of minutes, *Miss Petula Perpetual-Motion* did not move a muscle.

After an hour of snooping, the headmistress leaped out from behind the shelves.

"AHA!" exclaimed the lady. "GOTCHA!"

"Shush!" shushed Petula, her eyes indicating a sign on the wall of the library that said

## SILENCE!

"But, but, but…!" The headmistress couldn't contain herself. "You can sit still if you **want** to!"

"Yes, I can!" replied the girl. "And I have ALWAYS been able to!"

"But what about that **letter** from your mother?"

"Oh, that silly old thing? I wrote that myself!"

"ONE HUNDRED **YEARS** OF DETENTION!"

bellowed

Miss Prigg.

"I'd love to, I really would, but today is my very **last** day at ⟩ *Modesty Place* ⟨. And for old times' sake I am going to...

# ...**cartwheel** out.
# Farewell, Headmistress!"

With that *Miss Petula Perpetual-Motion* leaped on to her hands and spun out of the library, sending every single book flying through the air.

THUD!

THUD!

THUD!

The headmistress was in the library until **midnight,** picking up all the books and putting them back on the shelves. Then she still had to mop up the vomit.

So now you know,

**Miss Petula Perpetual-Motion**

really was one of the world's **worst** children.

## WONDERFULLY

so.

THE END

# CARTWHEEL CHAOS

Can you spot five differences between these two pictures of Petula?

ANSWERS ON PAGE 60

# DO THE JIGGLE!

Draw and colour your own character who loves to jiggle and joggle like Petula.

# CRASH! BANG! WALLOP!

Can you find the words CRASH, BANG and WALLOP in the grid? (Hint: they all appear twice.)

```
W  C  R  A  S  H  H
B  A  N  G  W  S
S  T  L  E  R  A
N  G  F  L  L  R
G  N  A  B  O  C
W  A  L  L  O  P
```

ANSWERS ON PAGE 60

# MAKE YOUR OWN BOOK

Did you love this book? Why not make your own? Pick an adjective and character from the lists below to choose your title.

**ADJECTIVES**

1. Magic
2. Mysterious
3. Mushy
4. Silly
5. Slimy
6. Smiley

PICK ONE

**CHARACTERS**

1. Mum
2. Monkey
3. Mammoth
4. Santa
5. Sister
6. Squirrel

PICK ONE

My book title is

.........................................

Using your title, design your brilliant book cover here.

TITLE HERE

YOUR LOVELY DRAWING HERE

AUTHOR NAME HERE

# ANSWERS

**SEARCH-AND-FIND ANSWER:** Modesty Place on page 3

## CARTWHEEL CHAOS

## CRASH! BANG! WALLOP!

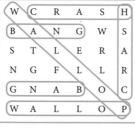

# David Walliams

## Miss PETULA Perpetual-Motion

Illustrated in
glorious colour by
**Tony Ross**

working in
partnership
with

National
Literacy
Trust

HarperCollins *Children's Books*

"Miss Petula Perpetual-Motion" from *The World's Worst Children*,
first published in Great Britain by
HarperCollins *Children's Books* in 2016

HarperCollins *Children's Books* is a division of HarperCollins*Publishers* Ltd,
HarperCollins Publishers
1 London Bridge Street
London SE1 9GF

The HarperCollins website address is
www.harpercollins.co.uk

Made for McDonald's in 2019

1

The National Literacy Trust is a registered charity no. 1116260 and a
company limited by guarantee no. 5836486 registered in England and Wales
and a registered charity in Scotland no. SC042944. Registered address:
68 South Lambeth Road, London SW8 1RL.

National Literacy Trust logo and reading tips copyright
© National Literacy Trust, 2019
literacytrust.org.uk

Batch No. 19966-01

Find out more about HarperCollins and the environment at
**www.harpercollins.co.uk/green**

Printed in China
THH
A44